Received on
DEC 08 2021
Green Lake Library

NO LONGER PROPERTY
SEATTLE PUBLIC LIBRARY

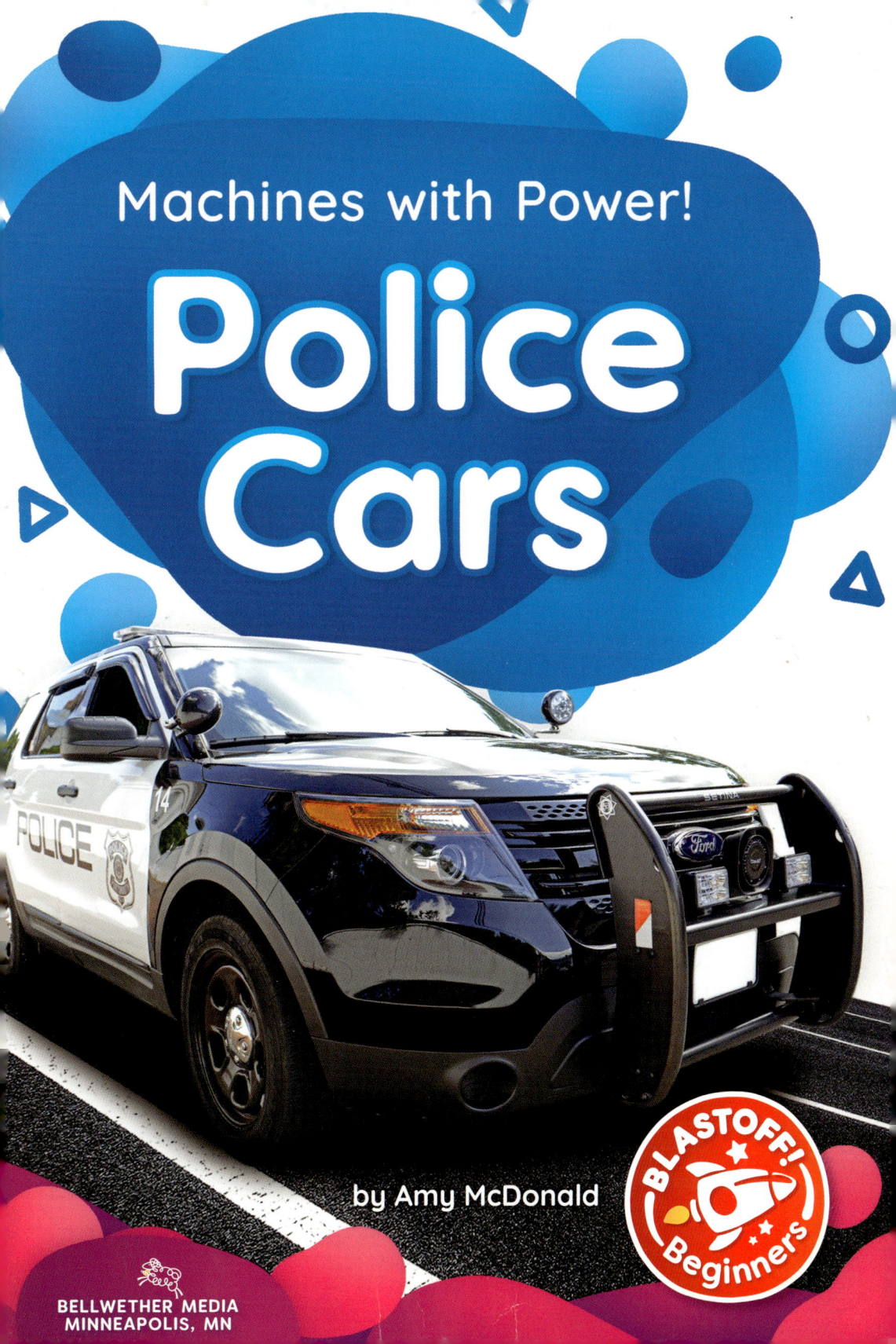

Blastoff! Beginners are developed by literacy experts and educators to meet the needs of early readers. These engaging informational texts support young children as they begin reading about their world. Through simple language and high frequency words paired with crisp, colorful photos, Blastoff! Beginners launch young readers into the universe of independent reading.

Sight Words in This Book 🔍

a	come	is	that	to
and	down	it	the	too
are	get	make	these	where
be	go	out	they	
blue	here	red	this	

This edition first published in 2022 by Bellwether Media, Inc.

No part of this publication may be reproduced in whole or in part without written permission of the publisher. For information regarding permission, write to Bellwether Media, Inc., Attention: Permissions Department, 6012 Blue Circle Drive, Minnetonka, MN 55343.

Library of Congress Cataloging-in-Publication Data

Names: McDonald, Amy, author.
Title: Police cars / by Amy McDonald.
Description: Minneapolis, MN : Bellwether Media, Inc., 2022. | Series: Blastoff! Beginners: machines with power! | Includes bibliographical references and index. | Audience: Ages 4-7 | Audience: Grades K-1
Identifiers: LCCN 2021003766 (print) | LCCN 2021003767 (ebook) | ISBN 9781644874783 (library binding) | ISBN 9781648343865 (ebook)
Subjects: LCSH: Police vehicles--Juvenile literature. | Police--Juvenile literature.
Classification: LCC HV7936.V4 M395 2021 (print) | LCC HV7936.V4 (ebook) | DDC 629.2088/3632--dc23
LC record available at https://lccn.loc.gov/2021003766
LC ebook record available at https://lccn.loc.gov/2021003767

Text copyright © 2022 by Bellwether Media, Inc. BLASTOFF! BEGINNERS and associated logos are trademarks and/or registered trademarks of Bellwether Media, Inc.

Editor: Christina Leaf   Designer: Andrea Schneider

Printed in the United States of America, North Mankato, MN.

Table of Contents

What Are Police Cars?	4
Parts of a Police Car	8
Police Cars at Work	16
Police Car Facts	22
Glossary	23
To Learn More	24
Index	24

What Are Police Cars?

Get off to the side! Here comes a police car!

Police cars are machines that stand out!

Parts of a Police Car

These are lights. They flash red and blue.

This is a **siren**.
It is loud.

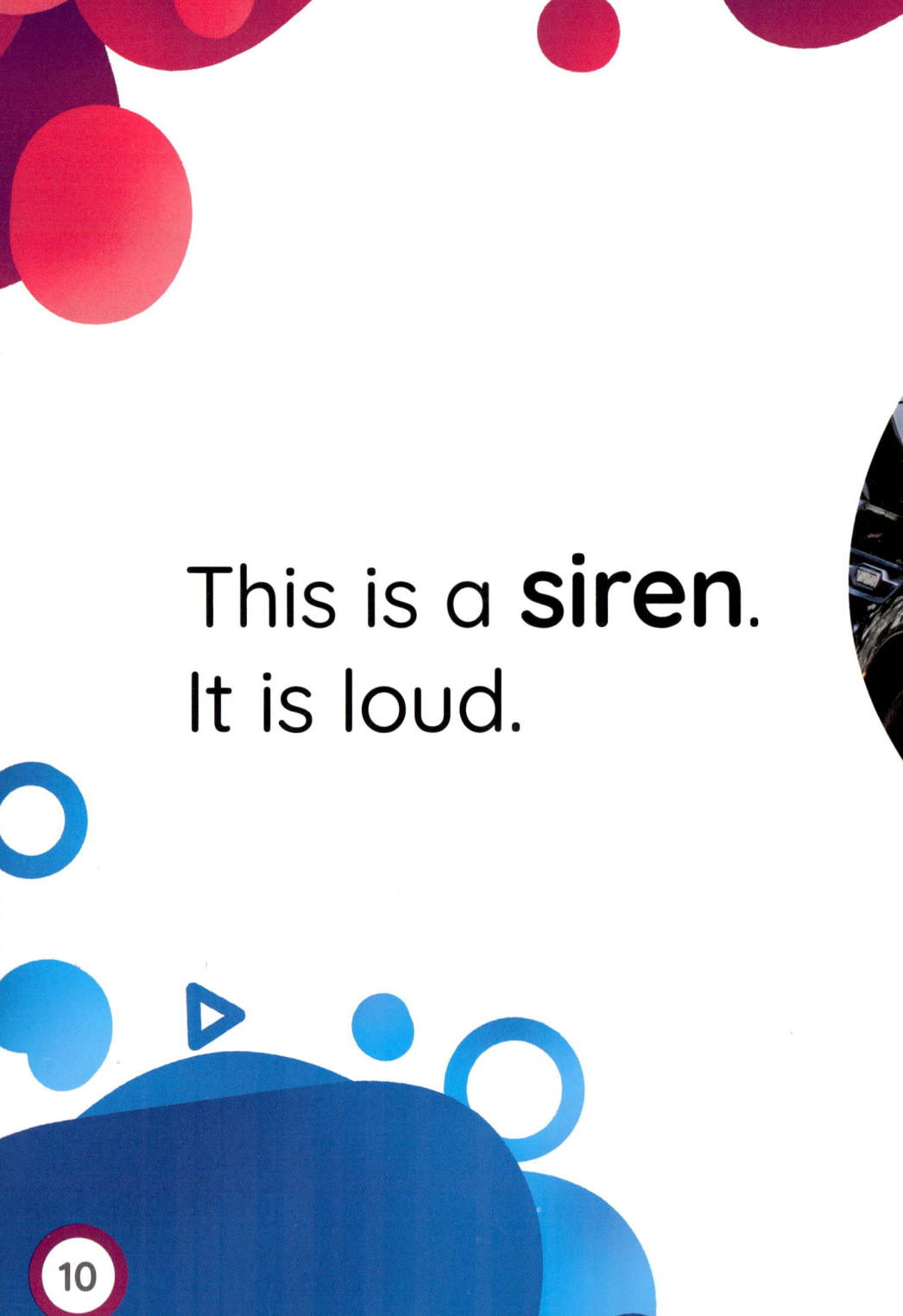

This is a **radio**. It tells police where to go.

radio

This is the **engine**. It makes police cars go fast!

engine

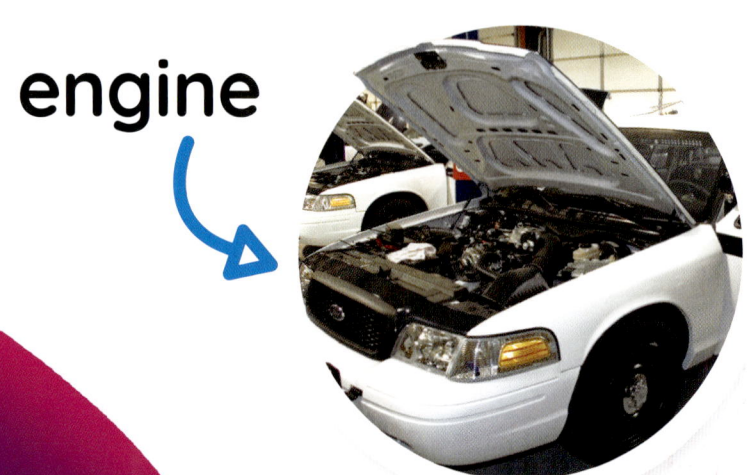

Police Cars at Work

Police cars bring **officers**. This car brings the police dog, too!

officers

This car blocks the road.
Be safe!

This car pulls someone over. Slow down!

Police Car Facts

Police Cars Parts

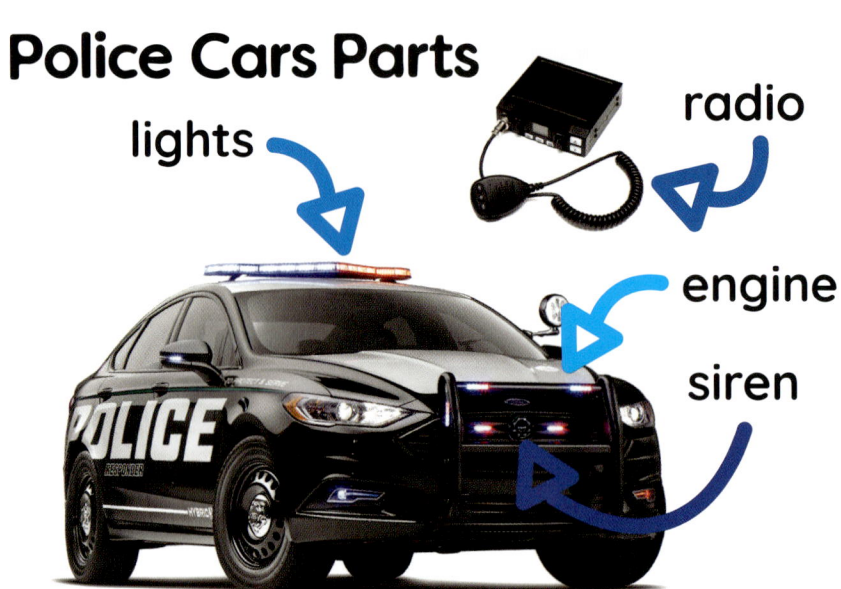

- lights
- radio
- engine
- siren

Police Car Jobs

carry officers

block roads

pull cars over

Glossary

engine

the part of a police car that makes it go

officers

people who work as police

radio

a tool to talk with other officers

siren

a tool that makes a loud sound to warn people

To Learn More

ON THE WEB

FACTSURFER

Factsurfer.com gives you a safe, fun way to find more information.

1. Go to www.factsurfer.com.

2. Enter "police cars" into the search box and click 🔍.

3. Select your book cover to see a list of related content.

Index

blocks, 18
blue, 8
bring, 16
engine, 14
lights, 8, 9
loud, 10
machines, 6
officers, 16
police, 12
police dog, 16
pulls, 20
radio, 12
red, 8
road, 18
side, 4
siren, 10, 11
slow, 20

The images in this book are reproduced through the courtesy of: Wangkun Jia, front cover; Fiat Chrysler Automotive, pp. 3, 4-5, 6-7, 8-9, 14-15, 16-17, 18-19, 22 (parts); Christopher A. Salerno, pp. 10-11; n_defender, pp. 12, 22 (radio); Lisa F. Young, pp. 12-13; David R. Frazier Photolibrary, Inc./ Alamy, pp. 14, 23 (engine); Sean Locke Photography, p. 16; Richard Peterson, p. 18; Mike Focus, pp. 20-21; Motortion Films, p. 22 (carry officers); V. Ben, p. 22 (block roads); Artem Avetisyan, p. 22 (pull cars over); a katz, p. 23 (officers); Yevhen Prozhyrko, p. 23 (radio); Radharc Images/ Alamy, p. 23 (siren).